I Like Flowers

written by Mia Coulton
illustrated by D.B. Campbell

I like to eat

red flowers.

3

I like to eat

yellow flowers.

I like to eat

orange flowers.

I like to eat

purple flowers.

I like to eat

pink flowers.

I like to eat flowers.

MaryRuth
BOOKS

ISBN 978-1-933624-73-0

90000>

9 781933 624730